IN THE GROOVE

by Christine Peymani

First published by Parragon in 2007
Parragon
Queen Street House
4 Queen Street
Bath BA1 1HE, UK

ISBN 978-1-4054-9163-1

Printed in the UK

CHAPTER 1

Sasha sat in the DJ booth at Stiles High, headphones on, jamming to the cool new tune she was blasting over the school's airwaves for her lunchtime radio show. As the last strains of the song faded out, she leaned into the microphone and exclaimed, "That was the latest solo track from my good friend Roxxi. Doesn't she totally rock?"

Outside the booth, her best friends Cloe, Jade and Yasmin grinned at her and gave her the thumbs-up through the glass. On days when Sasha did her radio show, they always brought their lunches and hung out at the radio station to keep her company. Sometimes they even joined her in the booth to do special segments, like 'Jade's Fashion Faves' or 'Yasmin's News &

Views'. Today, Jade was helping out as Sasha's producer, making sure everything ran smoothly while Sasha worked her musical magic.

But for her final segment of the day, Sasha had an extra-special guest that not even her best friends knew about.

"Now join me in welcoming the ultra-cool Carmen Summers, whose hot new label, Groove Records, is launching next month."

Carmen strutted into the studio

looking totally glam in hipster jeans and a cool metallic tank. She slid into the chair beside Sasha and cooed, "Thanks for that awesome introduction."

"It's a total thrill to have you here," Sasha replied. "And word is that you have an exciting announcement to make here on KSTYLE, the voice of Stilesville!"

"That's right, Sasha," Carmen agreed, flashing a bright smile at her host. "At Groove Records, we're totally committed to launching the hottest talents of tomorrow, and that's why we're conducting a nationwide talent search to find America's coolest new pop stars."

"That sounds amazing!" Sasha exclaimed.

"It really will be," Carmen continued. "We'll be holding auditions all around the country this week. We'll fly the finalists to Chicago and the winning act will get a record deal with Groove. In fact, they'll be helping us launch our new label with a spectacular concert tour!"

"Wow," Sasha sighed. "That would really be a dream come true."

She met her friends' eyes through the glass of the DJ booth and had to smile – they were jumping up and down and looked as thrilled as she felt! But she kept her cool so she could finish off her broadcast. "What else can you tell us about the contest?"

"Well, we're looking for both groups and solo acts – basically anyone with a fresh new sound that can get the fans totally pumped," Carmen added. "And we'll be doing a round of auditions right here in Stilesville!"

Jade gestured to Sasha that her time was almost up and Sasha quickly wrapped up. "Thanks for sharing that fabulous scoop! And remember, Stilesville, you heard it here first! This is Sasha, wishing you a totally musical day!"

On the other side of the glass, Jade flipped a switch and ended the broadcast. Then she, Cloe and Yasmin burst into the booth and surrounded Sasha and Carmen.

"Groove is gonna be the hottest label ever," Cloe gushed, "I just know it!"

"I hope you're right," Carmen replied with a laugh. She glanced at her watch and added, "Sasha, I've got to run, but thanks again for having me on." Looking around at all four girls' eager faces, she continued, "And hey, I loved your Rock Angelz album. It would be awesome if you girls would compete."

"We're there!" Cloe cried as Carmen hurried out of the studio, giving the girls a little wave over her shoulder as she left.

"How cool is that?" Cloe squealed. "Sasha, did you know about this?"

Sasha shook her head, looking distracted.

“We have got to win that record deal,” Jade cried. “It’s the perfect chance to make our mark on the pop-music scene!”

“And don’t forget that fabulous cross-country tour,” Yasmin added. “We’ll get to see all sorts of awesome sights.”

“We were such a hit as the Rock Angelz that we’ll have no problem nabbing this prize,” Jade declared. “It’s almost not fair to the other groups!”

“Well, at least you don’t have a confidence problem,” Yasmin teased.

Jade shrugged. “Hey, when you’re good, you’re good!” She turned to Sasha, who had been strangely quiet through this whole exchange. “Right, Sash?”

“Pop music is a lot different from rock,” Sasha replied. “And Groove is definitely looking for a pop sensation. We’ll need a totally new sound to win this contest.”

“Okay, so when do we start working on

our sound?" Cloe asked. "I'm ready to do whatever it takes to snag that record deal!"

"Umm, I don't know," Sasha said, flipping through a pile of CDs on her desk. "Wow, it's really a disaster in here. I'd better restore some order before I head to class. We'll figure the rest of it out later, okay?"

She started arranging the discs alphabetically on the shelves that lined the walls of the studio, while her best friends exchanged worried glances. Sasha had always been into organizing her space, but how could she be focused on alphabetizing CDs when they had a singing contest to win?

"Do you want to meet after school to start brainstorming song ideas?" Yasmin suggested.

"Or hit the mall to come up with a hot new look?" Jade chimed in.

"Oh... I think I might be busy," Sasha

told them. "But I'll let you know later. Or, you know, you can get started without me and I'll catch up if I can."

"Okay... sure," Yasmin agreed.

Sasha was too busy straightening the pens on her desk to notice the concerned expressions on her friends' faces.

"Guess we'll see you later, then," Cloe called as she and the girls headed out of the DJ booth.

"What?" Sasha asked, finally looking up at her friends. She seemed super distracted. "Um, oh yeah. See you later."

As soon as the door of the radio studio closed behind them, Jade, Cloe and Yasmin darted over to their lockers to talk over what had just happened.

"Okay, what's wrong with Sasha?" Cloe demanded.

"I don't know, but it's got to be big," Jade replied. "I mean, she didn't even want to come up with a plan. And if there's one thing Sasha loves, it's making plans!"

"Totally," Yasmin agreed. "I don't know, girls. Do you think maybe she doesn't want to audition?"

"Maybe she thinks we shouldn't have to, since we've already had our own rock band," Jade suggested.

"But this is a totally different thing!" Cloe protested. "Sasha said so herself."

The bell rang and the girls all hurriedly grabbed books from their lockers while shoving others back onto the shelves.

"Let's meet up after school anyway," Cloe suggested. "I'm sure we can figure it out then."

"Sounds like a plan," Jade agreed.

Yasmin nodded, then called, "Gotta run – don't want to be late for class!"

The girls all dashed in opposite directions to make it to their classes. Behind them, Sasha wandered out of the radio studio, still looking dazed and slowly headed down the corridor alone.

"Great radio show today, Sasha," her friend Dylan said in their choir class. Dylan sat right behind Sasha's alto section with the rest of the tenors and she had turned around in her chair to chat with him while Ms Van Zandt, their teacher, worked on a part with the sopranos. "And what an awesome announcement! You and the girls are trying out, right?"

"Maybe," Sasha replied. She turned back around, staring at the chalkboard at the front of the room while she waited for Ms Van Zandt to begin working with the whole choir.

Dylan tapped on her shoulder to get her attention again. "Whoa, I didn't think 'maybe' was in your vocabulary. What's the deal, anyway?"

Sasha glanced over her shoulder at her friend and shook her head. "Nothing. I just haven't decided yet, okay?"

"Well, maybe the boys and I will have to take our shot," Dylan said. "I mean, I wouldn't want to crush you girls if you're going for it, but if not, we guys are ready to rock the house." He turned to his friend Eitan in the seat next to him. "Right, Eitan?"

"I could go for that," Eitan agreed. "You girls really aren't planning to try out?"

"Oh, I'm trying out," Sasha replied. "But I can't speak for the other girls."

"I'm sure they'll want to," Dylan told her. "I can't believe you girls didn't talk about it yet!"

“We talked about it. But we haven’t had time to decide anything,” she said.

“Is something wrong?” Eitan asked worriedly. “Do the girls not want to try out or something?”

“You can be the front man – er, girl – for our boy band, if you want,” Dylan offered. “I’m sure we could make great music together.”

“That’s sweet, Dyl,” Sasha replied. “But that’s not the problem. I mean, I think the girls would be into auditioning. I’m just not sure if I want to.”

“But Sasha, music is your life!” Eitan cried. “I can’t believe you’d give up an awesome opportunity like this!”

Sasha sighed. She didn’t know how to explain her dilemma to the boys. But luckily, Ms Van Zandt interrupted their conversation before Sasha had to try.

“Let’s run through that song with the

whole choir this time," their teacher called.

Facing the front, Sasha lost herself in the harmonies of the song they were working on for their next concert. She loved hearing everyone's voices weave together into one single, gorgeous sound – and she loved how the music could totally carry her away from all her worries.

After practice, Sasha tried to escape the room before the boys could ask her anything else. She watched Dylan run off after one of the sopranos and had to laugh to herself – Dylan was always chasing after one girl or another.

Sasha was relieved that she'd avoided an uncomfortable conversation. But then she felt a hand on her arm and whirled to see Eitan standing behind her, looking worried. "Are you sure you're okay, Sasha?"

As their classmates swept past, Sasha tried to come up with an answer, but couldn't think of anything to say. Soon they were the only ones left in the classroom apart from Ms Van Zandt, who was shuffling through sheet music back in her office. So finally, Sasha decided to tell him the truth.

"You have to swear not to tell anyone, okay?" Sasha began.

"Sure, if that's what you want," Eitan agreed immediately. "My lips are sealed."

"Well... I feel terrible about this, but..." Sasha drew in a deep breath, then finished in a rush, "but this time, I just really want to try doing a solo act."

"Wow," Eitan murmured. "I mean, I'm sure you'd be amazing at it. But won't the girls be gutted?"

"That's why I can't tell them," Sasha replied. "They'd never forgive me."

"Sure they would, if that's what you really want to do," Eitan insisted.

"You don't understand. We do

everything together. Everything," Sasha explained. "And the girls are already all pumped up about auditioning. I can't bail on them now."

"But you said nothing was decided yet, right?" he asked.

"Well, yeah, but I think the girls kind of just assumed," she said.

"Sasha, you have to do what's right for you," Eitan told her. "You know your friends will stand behind you, no matter what."

"Thanks, Eitan," Sasha replied. "I hope you're right."

She gave her friend a quick hug and he added, "Let me know if there's anything I can do, okay?"

"Okay." Sasha gave him a small smile as he headed out of the choir room. After a moment, she followed him into the corridor and hurried to her next class. She was glad she'd talked to Eitan, but she still didn't have any idea how she was going to tell her friends that she was breaking up the group – or if she could even bring herself to tell them at all.

CHAPTER 2

After school, Cloe, Jade and Yasmin met up at Cloe's car. "Is Sasha coming?" Jade asked.

"I don't think so," Cloe replied. "I just got a text message from her saying she had an extra choir practice, or something."

"Should we wait for her, then?" Yasmin suggested. "I mean, if we're going to start planning our act, it seems wrong to do it without Sasha here."

"Honestly, she didn't seem that into it," Jade said. "I kind of got the impression that she wouldn't care if we just auditioned without her."

"That's crazy!" Yasmin climbed into the back seat of Cloe's car, leaving the passenger seat for Jade. "Sasha's all about singing. Why would she pass up a huge chance like this?"

Cloe started the car and headed for the mall. "I don't know – maybe she's tired of performing."

"That doesn't sound like Sasha," Yasmin insisted, shaking her head. "I really think something's wrong."

"Well, maybe it's not performing Sasha's tired of," Jade chimed in. "Maybe it's performing with us that she's tired of."

"Oh my gosh, do you think she's ditching us?" Cloe cried. "We can't

perform without Sasha! She's our driving force, our inspiration. We'd be lost without her!"

She was so upset that she swerved slightly and Jade grabbed the wheel.

"Cloe! Keep your eyes on the road," Jade shouted.

"I am! I just got worked up for a second," Cloe told her.

"Look, there's no sense in jumping to conclusions," Yasmin said reasonably. "Why don't we just ask Sasha what's going on?"

"Yeah, but first we have to get her to talk to us," Jade pointed out. "Which she doesn't really seem to want to do."

She stared out of the window as Cloe pulled into the Stilesville Mall car park.

"Well, we'll see her at lunch tomorrow, anyway," Yasmin replied. "We'll get the scoop then. And in the meantime, there's no reason to spoil a perfectly good shopping trip with worrying."

"Good point!" Cloe agreed.

The girls hopped out of the car and scurried into the mall.

"I think we need a new look before we can come up with a new sound," Jade declared. "Right, girls?"

"Absolutely," Cloe agreed. "And we'd better get started, because I don't have a clue what we should wear – much less what we should sing!"

"I heard they're having a sale at 2-2-Much," Yasmin offered. "Should we start there?"

"Let's do it!" Jade declared.

The girls swept into the shop and Cloe immediately honed in on an adorable flared denim mini.

"Is this not the cutest skirt you've ever seen?" she squealed, hugging it to her chest.

"It's pretty adorable," Yasmin agreed. She browsed through the accessories rack at the front of the shop and scooped up a long, shimmery silver scarf. She flung it dramatically around her neck and struck a pose. "Well? How do I look?"

"Fabulous!" Jade cried. She snagged a long strand of gold beads that had been hanging next to Yasmin's scarf and draped it around her neck. "What do you think?"

"They're totally you!" Cloe squealed. "But you guys, don't you think you should find an outfit before you start picking out accessories for it?"

"You're right, you're right," Jade admitted. "But can you blame us for falling for these super-cute accessories?"

"No," Cloe admitted. "In fact, I might grab a few things for myself, while we're over here." She chose a skinny periwinkle scarf and a dangly gold necklace. "These will look fabulous with my new skirt!"

"Okay, but what top are you planning to wear?" asked Jade, their resident fashion expert. "Because all those accessories could look totally over-the-top if you don't pick something understated to pair them with."

"What about this?" Yasmin suggested, holding up a silk-screened black tee.

"Perfect!" Cloe exclaimed. "I'm gonna look like the hottest pop star ever to hit the stage!"

"We all are," Yasmin reminded her gently. "Now, help us find the right threads to do just that."

"Jade, I think this turquoise miniskirt would look fabulous on you," Cloe said, grabbing a skirt from the same rack where she'd found hers. "It would totally bring out your eyes!"

Jade turned to check out her friend's find and gasped. "Oh my gosh, I just grabbed a shirt in that exact same colour! It's meant to be!"

“Oh, but you won’t want a whole outfit in just one colour, will you?” Cloe asked, disappointed. Jade was always so good at finding cool looks for her friends that Cloe had really been hoping to help her put an outfit together, for once.

“Actually, this cream-coloured vest would add just the right touch to pull it all together,” Jade replied. “I really think it’s time for vests to make a comeback.”

Her friends smiled at each other – when Jade predicted a new fashion trend, she was always right. Soon they’d be seeing vests in all the fashion shows and magazines for sure.

“Good find, Cloe!” Jade added.

“Aww, thanks, Jade,” Cloe said with a grin.

"Okay girls, not to break up the miniskirt trend, but I have to have these jeans," Yasmin declared, holding up a pair of dark-blue skinny jeans. "But I know we need a unified look for the group. Is there any way these could work?"

"Definitely!" Jade declared. "I mean, we don't want to look like total clones! We just need to be on the same fashion wavelength." She looked approvingly at the jeans and scarf in Yasmin's arms. "Which we absolutely are!"

"Ooh, Yas, what about this tank?" Cloe asked, holding up a sky-blue tank top. "This shade would look gorgeous against your hair."

Yasmin took the top from her friend and held it up, checking herself out in a nearby mirror. "You're right, Cloe! You are on a total fashion roll today! But I still feel like I need a little something more..."

"How do you feel about hats?" Jade

called from across the shop. She held up a floppy lavender hat and Yasmin scampered over to try it on.

Yasmin plopped the hat on her head and posed for her friends. "Well? Is it me?"

"Yasmin, you look so hip!" Cloe squealed. "I can't wait to see you decked out in the whole outfit!"

"I think I'll finish it off with this silver belt," Yasmin suggested. "What do you think, Jade? Jade?"

She turned and saw that Jade had wandered halfway across the shop and stood mesmerized by a fuchsia jersey dress with a short, flared skirt. Yasmin motioned to Cloe and they both joined their friend, their arms full of their cute new finds.

"What is it, Jade?" Yasmin asked. "I thought you'd already found your look."

"Yeah... but wouldn't this be perfect for Sasha?" Jade murmured.

"Oooh, yeah!" Cloe agreed.

"But Jade, if she doesn't even want to perform with us, won't she be upset if we pick out an outfit for her to wear onstage?" Yasmin pointed out.

"Maybe... but how could she resist, if we gave her such a beautiful dress?" Jade replied.

"Oh my gosh, and this matching faux-fur shrug!" Cloe exclaimed, holding up her find from a nearby rack.

"She would look incredible in that," Yasmin agreed.

"Let's get it!" Cloe cried. "She'll love it, I just know it. And if she is thinking of leaving us – well, maybe this will help change her mind. Or at least, you know, make her think twice."

"Cloe, that's awful!" Yasmin protested. "We are not going to bribe our friend to audition with us!"

"But it's perfect for her," Jade said quietly. "Whether she sings with us or not, she's got to have it."

Yasmin looked from Cloe, clutching the fuzzy shrug, to Jade, with the silky sheath draped over her arm and took in the serious, pleading expressions on both girls' faces.

"Okay," Yasmin agreed. "Let's do it."

"Yay!" her friends cheered, as they all bustled towards the checkout queue.

"But she's going to need this, too," Yasmin declared, grabbing a chunky silver chain from the accessory display at the front.

"Good call, Yasmin!" Jade said.

The girls paid for their cool new threads, splitting the price of Sasha's outfit three ways, then burst back into the mall again.

"I hope she likes it," Cloe murmured.

“She will,” Jade promised.

“Let’s go and find her and show her our new outfits!” Cloe said eagerly.

“Not yet,” Jade replied. “We still need to put the finishing touch on our looks.”

“What else could we possibly need?” Yasmin asked.

“Boots!” Jade declared. “I see us all in fabulous, knee-high boots!”

The girls dashed into the shoe shop, where Jade found tall, creamy boots to match her vest, Yasmin picked out fur-trimmed boots in the same blue as her tank top and Cloe chose white, gold-studded boots for herself, plus a similar pair for Sasha.

“You were right, Jade – these boots are just what we needed,” Cloe exclaimed as they headed out to the car.

“And when we strut onstage in them, we’re gonna stomp all over the

competition!" Jade predicted.

The girls giggled as they piled into Cloe's car with their shopping bags strewn around them, certain that they were on the right track to winning the contest.

The girls couldn't get hold of Sasha that night, so they spent the next morning at school waiting anxiously through their classes, eager to present Sasha with her new outfit at lunchtime. Usually, the girls all rode into school together, but Sasha had called Cloe that morning to say she was running late and would drive herself.

"Running late is not like Sasha," Cloe said worriedly to Jade and Yasmin.

After her maths class that morning, Cloe gathered up her books and hurried into the corridor as the bell rang. She couldn't wait to get to her usual lunch table to get the scoop on what was up with Sasha. But first, she swung by her locker to grab the shopping bag filled with Sasha's gorgeous new outfit. She thought lunch would be the perfect time to present their gift.

When she entered the cafeteria, she immediately spotted her best friends, already clustered around their favourite table, happily talking and eating. Cloe was relieved to see that Sasha was there too – she'd been afraid that her friend would avoid them again, as she seemed to have been doing ever since her broadcast the day before.

Cloe pulled up a chair and slipped the shopping bag under it. She wanted to wait for just the right moment to reveal their fabulous fashion finds to Sasha.

"So we had a very successful shopping trip last night," Jade announced.

"Good," Sasha replied, keeping her eyes focused on her lunch tray. She bit into her sandwich and chewed slowly.

Undaunted, Yasmin added, "We found a whole new look we can use for our audition!"

When Sasha didn't say anything, Cloe chimed in, "We even found the perfect outfit for you!" Cloe wasn't convinced that this was the right time to reveal their finds, but she forced a smile and pulled out the purple shopping bag from 2-2-Much. "Ta-da!" she exclaimed, holding up the dress and trying to sound more cheerful than she felt.

"Oh wow," Sasha gasped. She reached for the dress and ran its soft fabric between her fingers. "It's absolutely fabulous. You guys – you bought this for me?"

"We knew you'd look totally glam in it," Jade explained.

"And that's not all!" Cloe added, encouraged by Sasha's reaction. "Check this out!" She handed Sasha the shrug, the necklace and the boots, Sasha looked increasingly stunned with each new item that Cloe revealed.

"Can't you just picture us grooving onstage in these awesome threads?" Cloe insisted. "We'll whip up a hip new sound that's bound to blow those judges away! And before you know it, we'll be zooming up the pop charts and playing concerts nationwide for all our adoring fans!"

Jade and Yasmin grinned at Cloe's outburst – she tended to get carried away, but that was what they loved about her. But Sasha remained strangely silent.

"You shouldn't have done all this," Sasha murmured at last, staring at the pile of clothing on her lap. “It’s really too much.”

“No, it’s 2-2-Much!” Cloe replied, trying to break the tension she felt mounting between them. When Sasha didn’t respond, she babbled, “You know, the shop? That’s where we got it, so–”

“Yeah, I get it,” Sasha said. With a sigh, she finally looked up at her friends. “Look, I think we need to talk.”

“Uh-oh, that sounds like trouble.” Jade tried to keep her tone light and playful, but her friends could tell she was seriously concerned.

“It’s just – I really don’t think I can accept this,” Sasha continued.

She tried to hand the clothes back to Cloe, but her friend backed away.

"You have to!" Cloe insisted. "They're totally you! Why, did you already pick something else for our audition?"

"That's the thing," Sasha began. "I don't think 'our' audition is going to happen."

"You're not trying out?" Jade cried. "But Sasha, it's an amazing opportunity!"

"It's not that. It's just – I kind of wanted to audition by myself this time. That's what I've been trying to work up the nerve to tell you."

She looked up sheepishly. Her best friends stared back at her, looking surprised and a little hurt.

"Why?" Cloe demanded. "Aren't we good enough for you any more?"

"You know you're amazing," Sasha replied. "It's just that I've never done the solo thing and I guess I just want to prove to myself that I can do it, you know?"

"So why didn't you tell us sooner?" Jade snapped. "Like, before we got all excited and came up with a whole new look for an audition that's not going to happen?"

"Please don't be angry," Sasha begged. "I know I should've said something sooner, but – well, I just didn't know what to say."

"You should absolutely try doing your own thing, if that's what you want," Yasmin said soothingly. From her spot between Jade and Sasha, she put a hand on each girl's arm to calm them down.

"Thanks, Yas." Sasha shot her friend a grateful look, then continued eagerly, "I mean, you girls know music is my life. And I have all these musical ideas that I've never been able to try, so–"

"I just don't see why you can't try them with us," Jade insisted. "What, you don't think we can live up to your high musical standards?"

"That's not it!" Sasha cried. "I love

performing with you girls and I know I'm going to miss it this time. But is it so wrong that, just this once, I want the spotlight all to myself?"

"You know what? That's just fine." Cloe turned to Yasmin and Jade and said, "But if you two wouldn't mind sharing the spotlight, would you like to audition with me? Because I have some awesome musical ideas of my own."

"I'm in!" Jade replied, but Yasmin paused, trying to read Sasha's expression.

"I'd like to – but only if you're cool with it, Sasha," Yasmin said.

"You don't need her permission!" Cloe cried.

"Yeah, just like she didn't need our permission to totally ditch us," Jade added.

"This isn't about you!" Sasha insisted. "It's about me trying to pursue my dreams. Is that so wrong?"

"No," Yasmin replied, "it's not." She looked meaningfully from Cloe to Jade. "Right, girls?"

"I guess not," Cloe muttered, whilst Jade nodded reluctantly.

"So do you mind if I try out with Cloe and Jade?" Yasmin asked.

"Go for it," Sasha said. "I mean, it's an open audition, so it's not like I can stop you."

"Well, there's a glowing endorsement," Jade complained, rolling her eyes.

"What am I supposed to say?" Sasha demanded. "That I'm thrilled to have my best friends competing against me instead of supporting me? Yeah, that's every girl's dream."

"Come on, Sash," Yasmin said. "You know we're excited about this audition, too. It's fine if you want to do your own thing, but how can you be cross with us for wanting to do ours, too?"

Sasha carefully replaced the new outfit in the shopping bag Cloe had given her, crumpled up her napkin and tossed it on her lunch tray and shoved her notebook into her corduroy messenger bag, all without saying a word.

"You're right," she admitted finally. "May the best girl win."

She tried to give Cloe the shopping bag, but Cloe still refused.

"That was a gift," Cloe insisted. "We're not going to take it back."

"Well... thanks," Sasha said, sounding embarrassed. "Sorry to eat and run, but I need to get to choir practice. See you girls later."

She tossed the remains of her lunch into a nearby bin, gathered her bags and hurried off.

The girls watched her go, then turned to

each other anxiously.

"Wow," Jade said, once Sasha was out of earshot. "That was not what I expected."

"I can kind of understand, though," Yasmin replied. "I mean, music is her thing. Like, I'd feel weird if you guys all entered a writing contest." Yasmin was known among her friends for her amazing creative writing talents. "Or Jade, you'd be gutted if the rest of us suddenly became the school's hippest fashion designers."

Jade nodded slowly.

"And I guess I wouldn't like it if you all decided to be artists," Cloe, the group's resident artist, admitted.

"So you can see why she'd want to branch out on her own, right?" Yasmin prodded them.

"I guess..." Jade agreed. Yasmin stared at Cloe until she nodded, too.

"But are we really going to compete

against her?" Cloe asked. "I mean, besides the fact that she's our best friend, she's really good! Do you think we even have a shot without her, or should we just give up now?"

"We've never given up before," Yasmin pointed out. "Why start now?"

"Yeah!" Jade cried. "Besides, we can't let those awesome new outfits go to waste!"

Cloe smiled at her friends, encouraged by their eagerness. "Okay, then. Should we start practising tonight?"

"Totally!" they cheered.

Cloe tried to share their enthusiasm, but couldn't. She just didn't know how they would pull things together without Sasha to lead the way.

CHAPTER 4

Cloe, Jade and Yasmin were having a great time hanging out at Cloe's place, but they had to admit that they weren't exactly getting much done.

Jade had suggested a fashion show of all their new outfits and the girls had been happy for the chance to show them off. They all agreed that they looked like real pop sensations!

Cloe had made smoothies for her friends and the girls lounged around her room, chatting while they enjoyed her fruity creations.

"Girls, aren't we supposed to be rehearsing?" Yasmin reminded them.

"We have plenty of time," Cloe scoffed.

Yasmin knew Sasha would have pushed

her friends to get on track, but Yasmin had never been forceful like Sasha was. So when Jade mentioned that she thought Eitan might have a crush on Sasha – she'd spotted them chatting after choir practice the past few days – the girls were soon sidetracked by speculation.

"Oh come on, I'm sure they're just friends," Cloe insisted.

"I don't know..." Jade replied, raising her perfectly arched eyebrows.

"Don't you think Sasha would tell us if something were going on?" Yasmin asked. Her friends turned to stare at her and she continued, "She still would, wouldn't she?"

The girls just shook their heads and after a moment they filled the awkward silence by changing the subject to something else.

They'd been hanging out for hours when Cloe glanced at the clock and gasped, "You guys, it's getting way late and we haven't done anything!"

"Okay, but how much can there be to do?" Jade asked calmly.

Her friends loved how chilled out she always was, but that didn't stop them from feeling anxious.

"Well, we have a big audition in a week and we don't have even one song ready," Yasmin pointed out. "That seems like kind of a problem."

"But Yasmin, don't you have something

we can use in your notebook?" Jade insisted.

Yasmin always carried her creative writing notebook around with her and it was filled with fantastic writing of all kinds, from short stories to poems to song lyrics.

"Well... I do have a couple of things," Yasmin admitted. "But they're still really rough, you know?"

"Come on, let's hear them!" Cloe exclaimed.

"Okay..." Yasmin took a deep breath, then sang, "Sitting here and feeling strong, on top of the world."

"That's awesome!" her friends cheered.

Encouraged, Yasmin started singing louder. When she reached the refrain for the second time, her friends chimed in, "All my girls shout it and express yourselves!"

They broke down in laughter, thrilled with their new sound.

“I love it!” Jade cried.

“It’s totally us,” Cloe agreed.

“I’m so glad you like it,” Yasmin replied. “So now we just need to figure out the musical accompaniment and the harmonies and...” She trailed off as her friends stared at her blankly.

“Umm... do you know how to do that stuff?” Jade asked hopefully.

“No,” Yasmin said. “Don’t you?”

“Sasha always takes care of all that!” Cloe complained. “She’s the musical one.”

“Well, it’s up to us now,” Jade reminded her. “But I’m sure we can figure it out, right, girls?”

“Maybe...” Yasmin said. “But I think it’s kind of complicated, you know?”

“Let’s worry about that later,” Cloe said impatiently. “For now, let’s hear what else you’ve got. We need three songs for the audition, right?”

"I think so," Jade agreed. "At least, if we make it all the way to the final round."

"Oh, we will!" Cloe declared.

"If we can get these songs together," Yasmin reminded them.

"When we get these songs together," Cloe insisted.

In the meantime, Sasha was alone in her room, poring over the notebook she'd filled with lyric ideas and listening to the mini digital recorder she'd used to tape herself singing snippets of new songs.

"Is that it?" she asked herself, flopping on her bed in frustration. She'd been sure that she had tons of brilliant material saved up, but it all sounded as if it was missing something.

"Well, they are just ideas," she reminded herself.

But she couldn't help feeling that,

without her friends to bounce those ideas off of, she'd never be able to turn them into something truly amazing.

While she lay on her bed feeling sorry for herself, her puppy, Tango, bounded into the room and leaped up beside her, licking her face encouragingly.

"Okay, okay," she said, giggling. "I get it – we have work to do, right, Tango?"

"Woof!" Tango agreed.

"See what you think of this," Sasha said.

She pulled out her guitar and strummed a few chords, then really started jamming. Tango wagged her tail excitedly, then ran over and tried to jump up on Sasha's lap. Sasha stopped playing and scooped up her puppy.

"I guess that means you like it, huh? Now if only I had Yasmin's lyric-writing skills to make it really pop. The stuff I scribbled down just can't compare." She stroked her puppy's head and asked hopefully, "Do you have any ideas?"

But Tango just stared at her owner with her big brown eyes wide.

"Yeah." Sasha sighed. "Me neither. Who knew going solo would be so hard?"

Tango jumped down again and Sasha stood up and wandered around her room, picking up photos of her and her friends – on a trip to Paris, playing a gig as the Rock Angelz and hanging out at the prom. In every picture, they looked so happy, so close, as if nothing could ever come between them.

She noticed her cordless phone lying on her desk and almost reached for it, wanting to call her friends and get their help like she always did. But she stopped herself with a shake of her head.

"I can do this," she reminded herself. "I mean, sure, it's an adjustment. But it's what I have to do if I ever want to launch my solo career. So I'll figure it out. I'll have to."

But she couldn't concentrate and when she had trouble concentrating, Sasha liked to organize. It made her feel calmer, more in control. In her hurry to start practising that evening, she'd dumped her book bag in a corner of her room and now she carefully unpacked it, arranging her books on her desk and her makeup bag on her dressing table. She hung up her denim jacket and under her jacket she caught sight of the purple shopping bag that Cloe had given her that afternoon.

She reached in and pulled out the fabulous dress her best friends had bought for her, the perfect shade to bring out the reddish highlights in her hair. She hugged the dress to her chest, picturing the eager look on Cloe's face when she had unveiled it – and her injured expression when Sasha announced that she wouldn't be wearing it onstage with her friends. Sasha had known the girls would be upset, but she'd never suspected that her desire to go solo might ruin their friendship. Now she was afraid that it had.

CHAPTER 5

When Eitan rang the doorbell at Sasha's house on Saturday afternoon, she was desperate for a break. She'd been experimenting with cool new rhythms and melodies, but she couldn't seem to find the sound that she'd imagined, a sound that would be totally her. She had thought that by going out on her own, she'd have the chance to become a true pop diva, or whip up some edgy hip-hop beats that would really make her stand out, but instead she was totally stumped.

"What's up?" she asked, surprised to see Eitan standing on her doorstep. They'd been friends for a long time, but they'd always hung out in a group. She couldn't remember him ever just dropping round before.

"I heard what happened when you told the girls you were auditioning solo," he explained. "And I thought you could use a little cheering up."

"I don't know, I have a lot of rehearsing to do–" Sasha protested, but Eitan held up a hand to stop her.

"Just a smoothie break," he insisted. "I promise, you'll come back totally refreshed and ready to tackle those tunes."

"That does sound good," Sasha admitted.

She followed Eitan down the driveway and hopped into his jeep for the drive to their favourite smoothie shop at the mall.

"You don't mind dropping in on your day off?"

Sasha asked.

Eitan worked at the smoothie shop to pick up some extra cash.

"Nah – it's the best place in town!" Eitan replied. "Why would I want to go anywhere else?"

They pulled up at the mall and headed for the food court, where Eitan ordered their favourite smoothies while Sasha found them a table. When Eitan strolled up and set Sasha's tall blueberry smoothie in front of her, she smiled gratefully.

"This was a great idea," she told him. "I'm really glad you convinced me to get out of the house."

Eitan smiled back and settled into the chair across from her. "I figured you could use a break from all that rehearsing."

"Yeah, well, mostly I needed a break from not rehearsing," she replied.

"What do you mean?" he asked. "Isn't

it going well?"

"It's not going at all," she admitted. "I'm not used to doing everything by myself and honestly, I don't think I'm good at it."

"Sasha, don't be silly!" Eitan cried. "You're good at everything you put your mind to. I know you can do this, if it's what you really want."

Sasha looked up from her smoothie, blushing a little. "That's really sweet," she said. "But you know, I'm not sure it is what I really want any more."

"Then tell the girls!" he urged her. "They'll be thrilled to have you back."

"I can't – not after I made such a big deal about needing to do my own thing." She took a long sip of her smoothie, then gave Eitan the determined look he was used to seeing on her face. "So I'll just have to figure this out. And you're right – I can do it, if I just try hard enough."

"That's the spirit!" he agreed.

"So what about you – did Dylan ever talk you into auditioning?" she asked.

"Actually – yeah," Eitan admitted reluctantly. "I've been meaning to tell you. You don't mind, do you?"

"Of course not! I'm all for a little healthy competition." Sasha gave him a half-smile and added, "Besides, I can totally take you!"

"Oh, we'll see about that!" Eitan replied with a laugh. "Dylan is pretty pumped up about this. He's convinced it's his destiny to have crowds of adoring fans."

"That is so Dylan," Sasha said, grinning. "So you're going to be one of his backing singers?"

"Yeah, something like that," Eitan agreed. "Cameron and I are just there to make Dylan look good."

"I'm sure you can manage that." Sasha

took a last slurp of her smoothie, then stood up quickly. "Well, now that I know I have such stiff competition, I should probably get back to work."

"If you say so," Eitan replied. He stood up and watched Sasha for a moment before adding, "But I really don't think you have anything to worry about."

Cloe, Jade and Yasmin walked by just then, taking a break from their stalled rehearsals at their favourite place to get inspired – the mall. When they spotted Sasha and Eitan chatting just feet away, all three of them did a simultaneous double take.

"Quick! Hide!" Cloe hissed, pulling her friends behind a sunglasses kiosk set up at the edge of the food court.

"Why are we hiding?" Yasmin demanded, crouching down behind the sunglasses racks.

"I don't want Sasha to think we're

spying on her," Cloe whispered.

"Um, Cloe?" Jade began. "I think hiding behind things and peeking out at people looks a lot more like spying than, I don't know, just walking by."

"She is clearly here on a date with Eitan, which she clearly doesn't want us to know about and she's already cross with us, so she'll definitely think we're following her!" Cloe exclaimed.

Yasmin and Jade exchanged a look. Cloe tended to blow things way out of proportion and once she got going, it was almost impossible to bring her back down to earth.

"I don't think that was a date," Yasmin murmured. "I think Sasha probably just needed a friend, right now."

Cloe shook her head. "I don't know about that. I mean, we aren't the ones who left her – she abandoned us." She craned her neck around the corner of the kiosk, trying to spot Sasha and Eitan. "I think they're going the other way," she announced. "If we move fast, we should be able to get out of here."

"I seriously doubt that Sasha would be surprised to see us at the mall," Jade pointed out.

"Well, exactly!" Cloe cried, then clapped her hand over her mouth, realizing she'd been too loud. She glanced around anxiously in case Sasha had somehow sneaked up behind them. In a softer voice, she continued, "If she sees us here, she'll know we can't finish any songs without her. And I don't want her to have the satisfaction."

"Cloe, I don't think she'd be happy to know we're struggling without her," Yasmin said. "I'm sure it would only make her feel worse about the whole thing."

"Um, sorry to interrupt, but can we please get out from behind this kiosk?" Jade asked. "The saleslady is starting to look at us funny."

She shot a smile in the direction of the saleslady, who was staring at the three crouching girls with her arms crossed, tapping her foot impatiently. Jade grabbed her friends by the arms and yanked them out of their hiding place.

"See?" she declared. "Coast's clear."

"Well, that's enough shopping for me," Cloe announced as they strode away from the food court. "We've got to get back to work."

"Enough shopping?" Jade asked, stopping in the middle of the hallway with a mock-horrified expression on her face. "No such thing!"

"Come on, we have to get in some more practise," Cloe protested. "We don't have anything ready yet and the audition's next Saturday!"

"But we haven't even bought anything yet," Jade teased, grinning at her friend. "We can't give up now."

"Jade!" Cloe protested, but then she noticed her friend's smile. "Oh, ha-ha. I know, it's so funny that I care about this audition. Let's all make fun of Cloe now."

"Cloe, come on," Yasmin said soothingly, pulling Cloe over to the side so they wouldn't get run over by other shoppers. "We all care about the audition. But we weren't exactly making huge progress back at your place."

"We always get fresh new ideas at the mall," Jade reminded Cloe. "I think we just need a little more time."

"No, we need a lot more practise!" Cloe wailed. "That's what we need."

"Maybe we already got our inspiration," Yasmin interrupted. Cloe and Jade looked at her, surprised, while crowds of people bustled past them. "We need Sasha," Yasmin explained. "Maybe seeing her here was, like, a sign. She looked gutted and I know we're gutted and I think we should stop driving ourselves nuts at rehearsals and spend our time doing whatever it takes to win Sasha back instead."

"Do you think we really have a chance?" Jade asked as they headed for the exit. "She seemed pretty determined to try a solo act."

"Okay, but what do you think wanting to go solo means?" Yasmin inquired.

"It means she wants the spotlight all to herself, like she said," Cloe replied.

"But even solo artists need a band, right?" Yasmin continued.

"Sure," Jade agreed. "I mean, it isn't an a cappella contest."

"So, maybe this time, as a favour to Sasha, we could let her be the lead singer," Yasmin suggested. "And we could be her backing band."

The girls burst through the mall's doors into the sunshine outside and hopped into Cloe's car.

"Do you think she'd go for that?" Jade asked.

"Are we going for that?" Cloe demanded. "I mean, this audition is important to me, too. I don't want to just dance around in the background while Sasha gets all the attention."

"Cloe, it isn't always about you!" Yasmin reminded her. Cloe loved being the centre of attention, but her friends knew that deep down, she cared more about her friends than she did about being in the limelight. "This is Sasha's dream and if we're really her best friends, we should help her make it come true."

"If she'll let us," Jade added.

Cloe clutched the steering wheel, staring through the windscreen at the rows and rows of brightly coloured cars that surrounded them.

After a long moment, she said, "Okay. Let's go and see if we can talk her into it."

CHAPTER 6

After Eitan dropped her off at her house, Sasha lay on her bed, staring at the ceiling, with tunes running through her head. As hard as she tried, though, she still couldn't seem to dream up anything that really worked. She was thinking about heading to the record shop – maybe grabbing some new albums would help spark her creativity. But just then the doorbell rang and she rushed to the door, eager for a distraction.

She flung open the door, but then stopped short, stunned to see Cloe, Jade and Yasmin standing on her front porch.

"Hey, Sasha," Jade said. "Can we come in?"

Sasha stared at her best friends for a moment, then stepped back and opened the door wider.

"Sure," she shrugged as her friends walked past her.

Cloe, Jade and Yasmin sat on the sofa, while Sasha perched on a chair opposite them.

"Well, what can I do for you?" she enquired coolly, watching them with narrowed eyes.

"We want to audition with you," Cloe burst out.

"We've been through this!" Sasha protested. "Just this once, I need to do my own thing. Why can't you respect that?"

"No, no, we understand that," Yasmin interjected, leaning forward in her seat. "But we figured you might be able to use a backing band, and we were hoping we could get the gig."

Sasha crossed her arms over her chest, refusing to meet her friends' eyes. But after a long pause, she said softly, "You would do that for me?"

"Absolutely," Cloe replied. "You said you wanted us to support you and we figured this was the best way to do it. So, would you be up for it?"

"I could use some help filling out my sound," Sasha admitted.

"Let's hear what you've got!" Jade exclaimed. The girls hurried to Sasha's room and grabbed spots on the floor and bed, while Sasha picked up her guitar and strummed a few chords before launching into a song.

"Can you handle my style, can you

handle my attitude?" she sang. The girls nodded encouragingly, but Sasha stopped singing, concentrating instead on playing her guitar with her eyes tightly shut. When she reached the end of the song she looked up anxiously. "That's all I've got so far."

"That's an awesome sound," Jade declared.

"Yeah, but I don't have any lyrics," Sasha said, embarrassed. "I'm just not good with words like you are, Yas."

"But those first lines were fantastic," Yasmin told her. "We can totally build on those."

"Really?" Sasha asked hopefully.

"Sure!" Yasmin replied. "It seems like you were trying to capture a real sense of individuality in this song, right?"

"Definitely," Sasha agreed. "It was supposed to be about, you know, what it's like going out on my own."

"Okay, cool." Yasmin looked thoughtful for a moment, then whipped out the mini notebook that she always kept in her purse to jot down ideas. She wrote quickly, crossed a few things out, read back over her notes, then suggested, "What about something like ''Cos I really wanna shine, every time, take the world by surprise and I'm ready to?'"

"Yas, that's perfect!" Sasha cried. "How'd you do that?"

"I just imagined how you must be feeling about developing your own sound and thought about what you said you wanted this song to express," Yasmin explained. "And combined with the tune you played for us, this just sounded right to me."

"It's exactly what I was trying to say," Sasha told her.

Yasmin kept jotting down lyrics, then showed Sasha her notebook.

"How's this for the rest of the song?"

Sasha scanned the lyrics and shook her head in amazement.

"That's incredible. I've been working on this song for hours and couldn't come up with anything. Then you spend a couple of minutes on it and come up with something brilliant!"

"Hey, you already had the music there, and the ideas," Yasmin replied modestly. "That's a huge part of it. I could never come up with a song like that in the first place. But if you need lyrics, I'm your girl."

"So can I hear the songs you girls were working on?" Sasha asked. "I'd love to use them for the audition."

"Yasmin has a really pretty song we were working on," Cloe offered.

"It's not finished, though," Yasmin said.

"Oh, yeah, and mine was?" Sasha teased. "Come on, let's hear it!"

Yasmin sang the song that she'd worked on with the girls the night before and halfway through, Sasha grabbed her guitar and started strumming a gorgeous harmony line.

"That's exactly what the song needed!" Yasmin cried. "Do you think you'd want to sing it for the audition?"

"Actually, I think you should sing it," Sasha said. "It's a perfect song for you."

"No way," Yasmin protested. "You wanted your shot at the spotlight and I'm not going to take that away from you. If you don't want to sing this song, let's work on a different one."

Sasha put her arm around Yasmin and said, "Look, this doesn't have to be 'The Sasha Show'. I tried going it alone and I realized that it's, well, pretty lonely. I missed you girls and honestly, I can't do this without you."

"We missed you too!" Cloe exclaimed, leaping up from her spot on the floor and pulling Sasha into a hug. "We were totally lost without you."

Soon Jade hopped off the bed and joined them in a group hug.

"We're just better together," Jade said and the others nodded in agreement. They stepped back and smiled at each other.

After a moment, Cloe asked, "Does that mean I can take the lead on a song, too?"

The girls laughed. Cloe really couldn't stand giving up centre stage.

"I think that could be arranged," Sasha agreed. "Yasmin, do you have any ideas?"

"I sure do!" Yasmin replied. Soon the girls were huddled together, happily whipping up another cool tune.

CHAPTER 7

When the girls pulled up to Stiles High on Monday, they were totally pumped about their new pop sound.

"We are gonna rock that audition!" Jade declared.

"Groove Records, here we come!" Sasha added.

But when they stepped through the front doors, they were shocked to see the walls plastered with posters for an all-girl band called the Chix.

"'Come and support your fave new band, the Chix, at their audition for Groove Records this Saturday'," Yasmin read. "Who are these guys, anyway?"

Dylan happened to be walking by and overheard Yasmin's question.

"Don't tell me you haven't heard of the Chix!" he exclaimed. "They gave this way-cool concert on Saturday that totally blew everyone away. I can't believe you girls missed it!"

"Yeah, well, we were practising for our audition," Sasha explained. "Aren't you guys trying out too?"

"Oh, yeah, we've been working on some stuff," Dylan said. "But after hearing the Chix perform, I'm not sure we should even bother. I mean, everyone's saying they're a sure thing to win!"

He paused, noticing the worried looks on the girls' faces. Dylan had a bad habit of saying whatever popped into his head without thinking first.

"Oops, sorry," he said. "I'm sure you guys have a great shot too. But really, you should hear this band!"

He dug through his rucksack and took out his MP3 player, pulling up a song by the Chix called 'All About Me', then handed his headphones over to the girls. They took turns listening and when the song was over, they all looked stunned.

"They're really, really good," Jade said.

"Now we'll never get that record deal!" Cloe cried. "All that work, for nothing!"

"Cloe, you don't know that," Sasha pointed out. "So we have some serious competition. That just means we have to work harder. Right, girls?"

Her friends nodded, but they didn't look at all convinced.

“Where did these girls come from, anyway?” Sasha asked Dylan.

“They’re from Pleasant Grove, two towns over,” he replied. “That’s where the concert was, but it was totally worth the drive!”

Sasha shot him a warning look and he backtracked quickly.

“You know, since you girls weren’t playing anywhere this weekend. They were, like, a good second choice.”

“Thanks, Dylan,” Jade said. “But you’re allowed to like other bands too, you know.”

“I’m so glad to hear you say that!” Dylan exclaimed.

He looked so relieved that the girls couldn’t help but laugh.

“Well, we’d better get to class,” Sasha said. “Thanks for giving us the scoop on this band.”

“Sure thing!” he replied. “Oh and if you

want to check them out yourselves, they're playing again tonight. I can't miss it – I think the lead singer likes me."

He winked at the girls and they giggled again.

"We'd love to go with you," Yasmin told him, "unless you think it would bother your singing sweetie if you showed up with a bunch of girls."

"Nah, that'll just show her how popular I am." Dylan ran a hand through his wavy hair, trying to look suave. "Meet me after school and we can head over."

"Sounds good!" Jade agreed, before they all headed in different directions to make it to their first classes before the bell rang.

All the girls could think about all day was the stiff competition they were facing right on their own patch.

"I can't believe we didn't know anything

about them," Sasha said at lunch. She munched on a carrot stick and shook her head. "I thought I knew all the bands on the local scene!"

"They must just be new," Jade suggested.

"Yeah and now they're totally taking over!" Cloe wailed. "I can't believe we wasted all that time competing against each other when we have this other band to defeat!"

Sasha looked hurt and Yasmin jumped in.

"It wasn't wasted, Cloe," she pointed out. "We came up with some awesome material and now we'll be better than ever!"

"But they'll have crowds of fans cheering them on at the audition," Cloe complained. "The judges are sure to go for them, since they'll already have a huge audience for their first album."

"So will we, Cloe," Sasha pointed out. "I mean, our Rock Angelz album was a huge success. I'm sure our fans will be excited to hear we're trying out a new sound."

"And people know us from Bratz Magazine, too," Jade added.

"Ooh and America Rocks Fashion!" Cloe chimed in, getting excited. "You're right – we're way better known than those girls!"

"Okay, Cloe," Yasmin said, laughing. "But we haven't even named our band yet. I think that might help out with the whole name recognition thing."

She took a long sip of her lemonade, then reached over and grabbed a crisp from Cloe's plate while the girls all

thought hard.

"I don't know," Cloe moaned after a few minutes. "I can't think of anything!"

"Okay, well, we want to be pop stars, right?" Yasmin began, looking thoughtful. "So what about 'Starz'?"

"Perfect!" Jade cried.

"Yas, you always come up with the best names," Sasha said. "I don't know what we'd do without you."

Yasmin shrugged modestly. "Luckily, you'll never have to find out."

"That's a great name," Cloe agreed. "But how are we going to get it out there so people will be cheering for us instead of those Chix on Saturday?"

"Why don't we give our own concert on Friday?" Sasha suggested. "It'll be great practise for us and it'll get us totally revved up for the audition on Saturday."

"Awesome idea!" Cloe cried. "But will

we have enough songs ready by then?"

"Girls, when we put our minds to it, anything's possible," Jade assured them.

After school, they met up with Dylan, Eitan and Cameron by their lockers.

"The boys couldn't resist the chance to spend a little time with you ladies," Dylan explained.

Cloe smiled shyly at Cameron. Those two really liked each other, but neither of them would ever make a move. Then Cloe noticed that Eitan was shooting Sasha a similarly infatuated look, but Sasha was totally oblivious.

She pulled Sasha aside and whispered, "Hey, is something going on with you and Eitan?"

"No," Sasha replied. "What made you think that?"

"Well, the way he's staring at you, for one thing," Cloe explained. "Plus we saw you two at the mall on Saturday and you looked pretty friendly."

"Yeah, because we're friends, Cloe," Sasha snapped. "Anyway, if you saw me there, why didn't you say hi?"

"You weren't exactly thrilled with us right then," Cloe pointed out. "I didn't think you'd want to see us."

"So you avoided me? That's just great." Sasha turned away, annoyed.

"Hey, girls, is everything okay?" Dylan asked, strolling over to them. "We should probably get going, if you're ready."

"We're fine," Sasha said, but her voice had a hard edge. "Just fine."

"Um, okay," Dylan replied, flustered. "Well, do you guys want to follow me, since I know the way?"

"Sure," Cloe agreed.

All seven friends headed for the car park, where the girls slid into Cloe's car while the boys got into Dylan's.

"See you there!" Dylan called out of his window before driving off.

Sasha sat in the back seat, staring out of the window in stony silence.

"What's wrong, Sash?" Yasmin asked, in the seat next to her.

"Nothing," Sasha replied.

Yasmin reached over and put her hand on Sasha's arm. "Seriously, what happened?"

Sasha turned to face her friend, eyes blazing.

"I just didn't realize that when I decided not to be in your band, you girls decided not to speak to me."

"That's not true!" Yasmin protested.

"We were just giving you a little space,"

Cloe added from the front seat. "We thought that's what you wanted."

"I didn't want to be totally abandoned, if that's what you meant," Sasha told them. "And if must know, I was hanging out with Eitan on Saturday because he was apparently the only one who wanted to be around me."

"We were rehearsing," Jade reminded her. "We assumed you were, too."

Sasha's expression softened. "I know," she admitted. "It's just – it was weird being away from you girls."

"It was weird for us too," Yasmin said, squeezing Sasha's arm.

"I'm glad we're back to normal," Sasha told her best friends.

"Totally!" the girls chorused, relieved that things seemed to be okay again.

"So you don't have a thing for Eitan?" Cloe insisted.

"No!" Sasha cried. "You know I'd tell you if I liked someone – you're my best friends."

"I know," Cloe replied. "It's just – I think he likes you."

Sasha thought back to how helpful Eitan had been to her ever since these auditions were announced — and she started to wonder.

"Nah," she said finally. "He's just being a good friend."

But she vowed to keep an eye on Eitan at the concert, just in case.

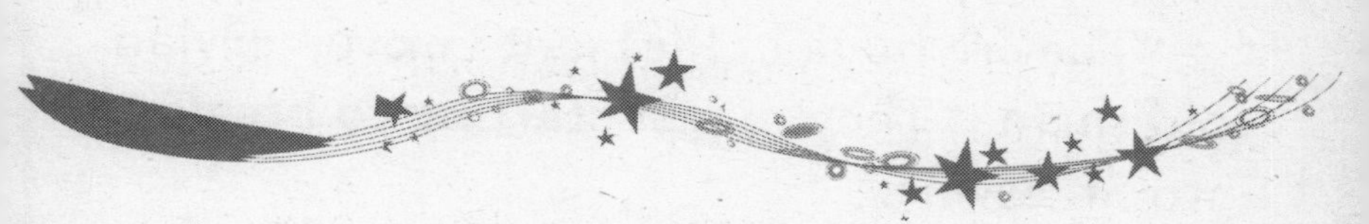

CHAPTER 8

When they arrived at the club in Pleasant Grove, there was already a long queue stretching out of the door. They had to park at the far end of the car park because it was already packed.

"This is unbelievable!" Cloe said as she slid out of the car.

"How did all these people find out about them before us?" Jade asked. "We're usually on the cutting edge of all the hottest trends!"

"They're huge in Pleasant Grove," Dylan told them. "They're just starting to break into Stilesville."

"See?" Sasha whispered to her friends. "We have nothing to worry about. We've played concerts in London and New York and they haven't even played outside of their home town!"

They joined the ticket queue, then filed into the club behind the huge crowd of teenagers and found a spot near the back of the room. Soon the band dashed onto the stage, dressed in jeans and sparkly tank tops.

"Hey, I'm Aimee and these are my girls, Ashleigh and Ally. And together, we are the Chix!" she shouted into the microphone.

The crowd broke into cheers as the Chix started playing. They opened with 'All About Me', the song the girls had heard that morning on Dylan's MP3 player, and it was even better in person. All three girls had gorgeous voices that soared above Aimee's guitar chords, Ashleigh's drumbeats and Ally's baseline.

They were upbeat and fun, and although Cloe, Jade, Sasha and Yasmin didn't want to like their competitors, soon they were dancing along to their tunes and having a blast.

"They seem cool," Cloe shouted over the music and her friends nodded.

"Maybe we can meet up with my girl after the show," Dylan yelled.

The girls laughed, sure it was just more of Dylan's talk, but when the concert was over, he led them confidently backstage.

"I'm with Aimee," he told the security guard who tried to block their way.

"I don't think we should be back here," Cloe said worriedly. Dylan might think he was charming, but Cloe was sure the stern-looking, muscle-bound guard didn't agree.

"I met Aimee after the last show and she asked me to come and see her tonight,"

Dylan assured her.

"We'll just see about that," the guard said, but just then, Aimee, Ashleigh and Ally appeared in the doorway of their dressing room. Aimee's face lit up at the sight of Dylan.

"Dylan!" she exclaimed. "I'm so glad you made it to the show!" She ran over and threw her arms around him, making him blush. "And who are your friends?" she asked as she pulled away.

"You met Cameron at the last show," Dylan began, "and then this is Eitan and my friends Cloe, Jade, Sasha and Yasmin."

"You girls were fabulous," Cloe gushed as she stepped forwards to shake hands with the Chix.

"They're actually competing against you at the Groove Records audition," Eitan announced.

"Really?" Aimee said, looking the girls

up and down. "Well, good luck to you."

"Yeah, you'll need it," Ally muttered under her breath.

"What was that?" Sasha demanded.

"Well, it's just, we were up there playing a show, while you were down there watching," Ally replied. "So who do you think is more likely to be named the hottest new pop star?"

"Hey, these are the Rock Angelz right here," Eitan protested. "Maybe you've heard of them?"

"Um, I don't think rock is really Groove's thing," Ashleigh told them. "You might want to try a different contest."

"No, we're a pop group now," Cloe explained. "We're the Starz."

"They don't look like stars to me," Aimee whispered to her friends, loud enough for the others to hear. Ashleigh and Ally sniggered.

"Okay then," Jade said. "I think we'd better get going."

"Yeah, you might want to use this time to rehearse," Ally suggested. "I'm sure you could use it!"

Cloe's eyes widened in shock at the girls' nasty words. Cameron, noticing how upset she was, stepped in front of her, as though shielding her from the rival band.

"Come on, Cloe, let's get out of here," he said.

Cameron led her away and the others

followed, until only Dylan was left facing the Chix.

"Bye," he said glumly to Aimee.

"Can't you stay?" she whined. "I was really hoping we could hang out."

"Sorry," he replied. "I can't hang out with someone who talks to my friends that way."

He hurried to catch up with his friends.

"I'm so sorry about that," he told them once they were outside. "She seemed so cool last time."

"We talked to her for, like, two seconds last time," Cameron pointed out. "I guess it takes her a little longer to get into full insult mode."

"Well, now we absolutely have to beat them," Jade declared. "Carmen seemed way too cool to have girls like that on her label."

"Oh yeah, those Chix are going down!"

Sasha agreed. "But they were right about one thing – we have some work to do."

As soon as they got home, Cloe designed a poster for the first-ever Starz concert, while Yasmin helped her write eye-catching text. Sasha called some local music venues she had worked with before and booked them at a cool club, while Jade dialled up her press contacts and got them to agree to cover the show.

Cameron dropped by to pick up the poster so he could make copies of it and Dylan and Eitan joined him in putting posters up all over town.

"It's really sweet of them to help us out, even though they're auditioning too," Yasmin said to the girls.

"Dylan just thought it would be fun to try out," Jade said. "I don't think the boys really care how they do. But they know it matters a lot to us, so they're happy to help out."

"They're the sweetest," Cloe agreed dreamily.

"Or at least one of them is, right Cloe?" Sasha teased.

"Oh, you must mean Eitan," Cloe replied with a grin. "He really does seem to like you, you know."

"Maybe so," Sasha said, "but right now, we have more important things to worry about. Like coming up with a full set so we can actually play this concert the boys are out there advertising right now."

The girls kept rehearsing, combining Yasmin's lyrics and Sasha's music to put together a full list of fabulous tunes. Then Sasha ran them through some dance moves so they could really sparkle on stage.

"Those Chix had better watch out," Jade declared as they wrapped up their rehearsal for the night. "'Cos the Starz are in town, and we're ready to shine!"

CHAPTER 9

The rest of the week was a whirlwind of whipping up new songs, rehearsing and trying to get the word out about their concert that Friday, in between going to school and doing their homework. By Thursday, the girls had an awesome set ready to perform and the town was covered with posters for their concert.

But that evening, as they ran through their set one last time, Cloe had a major meltdown. She kept forgetting the words to Yasmin's latest song – and mixing up the dance moves Sasha had choreographed.

"I can't take it any more!" she wailed finally, collapsing dramatically on the floor of Sasha's room. "We'll never be ready in time, everyone will laugh at us and the Chix will trample all over us at our audition!"

Sasha crouched on the floor beside her friend and put her arm around Cloe comfortingly.

"It's going to be okay," Sasha promised.

"We've made amazing progress already this week," Yasmin added, settling in beside her friends.

"We just have a little polishing left to do," Jade chimed in, joining the others on the floor, "and then we'll be ready to blow the competition away!"

Cloe held her head in her hands, refusing to look up at the girls. "We should have just let you audition alone," she whispered to Sasha, her voice muffled beneath her hands. "I feel terrible that

I'm ruining your chances."

"Cloe, I couldn't do this without you, remember?" Sasha assured her. "I need you guys too. And together, I'm sure we'll get way further than we ever could have alone."

"Totally!" Yasmin exclaimed. "Because we make an awesome team!"

"When the four of us are together, we can do anything," Jade agreed.

Cloe finally met her friends' eyes. "That's true..." she murmured.

"See?" Sasha cried. "Now come on, let's run through it one more time before we take a pizza break."

"You didn't tell me there was pizza at the end of the tunnel!" Cloe said, her blue eyes sparkling as the worried lines disappeared from her face. "With that kind of incentive, I can definitely get through this song."

Yasmin smiled down at Cloe as she

stood up, then helped her friend up from the floor. "That's our girl."

Sasha picked up her guitar. "Ready?" she asked. The girls all nodded and Sasha counted down, "And a-one, two, three!"

The girls burst into song and this time they were all totally perfect – not one of them missed a step or forgot a word.

"Never underestimate the power of pizza," Jade said with a laugh.

She whipped out her mobile phone and speed-dialled the local pizza place, ordering a couple of pizzas piled with their favourite toppings.

"This is definitely a well-earned break," Cloe sighed, flopping across Sasha's bed.

"Yeah, we were on for that last song," Sasha agreed.

"I can't wait for our concert tomorrow!" Jade added.

The girls could barely sit still during their classes the next day because they were so excited about their concert. Right after school, they headed to the club Sasha had booked to start setting up, and to run through a dress rehearsal onstage.

Their set went perfectly and by the time they'd practised each of their songs, they were totally pumped up to perform.

"Do you think many people will come?" Cloe asked. "We threw it all together so fast that I'm worried people didn't have time to find out about the performance."

"With how many posters the boys put up for us and all those calls we made, I'm sure people know," Jade pointed out. "Now the question is, will they show up?"

"How could they miss the debut of Starz?" Sasha cried. "It's the biggest concert of the month!"

"According to famous Stiles High DJ Sasha, anyway," Yasmin teased.

Sasha had devoted a big part of her radio show that week to talking up their concert.

"Hey, it's just true," Sasha replied. "I have a duty to my audience to alert them to all the hottest concerts. I can't help it if one of them happens to be ours!"

The girls headed backstage to change into the cute outfits they'd picked out for their audition – they thought they might as well preview their new look

©MGA

tonight. By the time they were dressed, their audience had already started filing in.

Cloe peeked around the edge of the curtain and squealed in excitement.

"There are tons of people out there already!" she exclaimed.

"Told you we'd have a good turnout," Sasha declared.

The girls did some stretches to limber up for their dance moves and Sasha led them in a few vocal exercises. Before they knew it, it was time to go on and they ran onstage while their fans cheered. They were thrilled to see that the entire club was packed!

Sasha grabbed the microphone and introduced the band, then started singing 'My Attitude', the first song she'd played for her friends after they reunited. The girls were totally in the groove and the audience started dancing along right away. When she finished the tune, Sasha took a bow, then stepped back to let Yasmin take the spotlight for her solo.

As Sasha looked out past the glare of the lights, she noticed Eitan jumping up and down in the front row, holding up a huge poster that read 'Sing It, Sasha & the Starz!'

She leaned over to Cloe and whispered in her ear, "Well, I guess you were right about Eitan." She nodded in the direction of the poster and Cloe giggled.

"I love it when I'm right!" she replied.

Then Yasmin's song started and the girls were strumming away, backing her up.

The girls had a blast singing all their new pop tunes and the audience was so into it that they cheered the girls on to three encores! Finally, the Starz had to sign off because they'd run out of songs. Besides, they needed to rest for their audition the next day.

"Goodnight everybody!" Sasha called to the crowd. "And remember, if you liked what you saw tonight, you'll love our Groove Records audition tomorrow, so come out and cheer!"

The audience burst into applause as the girls waved goodbye and hurried off the stage. They were so thrilled at the crowd's response that they almost didn't notice the three girls waiting for them backstage, arms crossed over their chests.

"Nice show," Ashleigh said with a smirk.

"Yeah, too bad you totally ripped off our sound!" Ally added.

"But don't worry, the judges will see right through your second-rate tunes to our true star quality," Aimee declared.

"How did you get back here, anyway?" Sasha demanded.

"What do you mean?" Aimee asked innocently. "We're friends of the band!"

"You have a strange idea of friendship," Yasmin replied. "See, we're not really into insulting our friends."

"Hey, we're just being honest," Ally told her, flipping her long red hair over her shoulders. "We wouldn't be very good friends if we weren't straight with you, now would we?"

Just then, Cameron, Eitan and Dylan hurried backstage.

"Awesome show!" Eitan exclaimed. Then he stopped, noticing the Chix glaring at his friends.

"Are these girls bothering you?" Cameron asked, shooting Cloe a concerned look.

"Nah, they were just leaving," Jade declared. "Weren't you, girls?"

"Whatever," Aimee grumbled. She turned to Dylan and demanded, "Are you sure you wouldn't rather hang out with a real band?"

"I already am," he replied.

"Humph!"

Aimee and her friends turned on their heels and stalked out through the back door. When they were gone, Jade grinned at her friends.

"Well, girls, I think we've got them running scared!"

"Definitely," her friends agreed.

CHAPTER 10

The night before the audition, the girls all slept over at Cloe's house so they could head over to the town's auditorium together for their audition first thing in the morning.

They all woke up early, too wired to sleep in, and ran through their three audition songs before hopping into Cloe's car and driving over to the auditorium.

"Whoa," Jade murmured when they pulled up and saw the huge crowd that had already gathered. "Do you think all these people are here to audition?"

"Hopefully they're all here to cheer us on!" Cloe exclaimed. But after they piled out of the car and made their way through the crowd, they discovered that over 100 groups had signed up ahead of them!

"And that's just in this region," Sasha pointed out. "Imagine how many people are going for this spot nationwide!"

They grabbed a row of seats at the back of the auditorium to wait their turn and soon the boys joined them to hang out until it was time to perform.

"So, are you ready?" Eitan asked, taking a seat next to Sasha.

"We were born ready!" she declared with a grin. "How about you guys?"

"Yeah, you know, we're just gonna go do our thing," Dylan replied. "If they like the Dudes, great. If not, that's cool too."

"I like that attitude," Jade said, reaching over to give Dylan a high-five. He was definitely

in line with her chilled-out vibe.

As the auditorium filled up, the girls were happy to see a lot of fans carrying signs with slogans like 'Go Starz!' and 'The Starz are #1!' But they were gutted to see a lot of signs supporting the Chix, too.

Soon Carmen appeared on the stage, along with two men who she introduced as fellow Groove Records execs Ian and Evan.

"Let's get the contestants lined up in order in the first ten rows," she began.

She read out the order of performances – the boys were going first and the Starz were last, right after the Chix.

"I can't believe we have to follow them!" Cloe complained.

"I can't believe we have to sit by them," Jade added as they headed towards their seats at the front.

"Good luck!" the girls chorused as the guys took the stage.

Eitan waved at Sasha, Cameron smiled shyly at Cloe and Dylan paused to wink at all four girls in turn.

"All right, first up we've got the Dudes," Carmen announced.

Dylan and the boys started to play and their friends cheered loudly from the audience.

"They're really good," Yasmin whispered to Cloe.

"Yeah, but they're no Starz," Cloe said confidently.

From her nearby seat, Aimee turned and snapped, "Neither are you."

Yasmin and Cloe just rolled their eyes at each other and finished listening to their friends' song. When the boys finished playing, Cloe, Jade, Sasha and Yasmin leaped up to give them a standing ovation.

"That was great, guys, but I just don't think you have the passion we need for our

Groove Records launch," the first judge, Evan, said once the applause had died down.

"I'll second that," the next judge, Ian, agreed.

"Good sound," Carmen added, "but definitely lacking that extra spark. Sorry, guys."

The boys looked a little disappointed, but they nodded, understanding where the judges' comments were coming from. When they stepped off the stage, though, a crowd of girls rushed forward, clamouring for Dylan's autograph.

Dylan's eyes instantly lit up. "Hey, hey, there's plenty of the Dyl-meister to go around!" he exclaimed.

"See, he got what he always wanted," Sasha said.

"A crowd of adoring fans?" Jade replied. "Yep, that's Dylan's dream come true."

"These judges are tough," Cloe pointed out anxiously. "I mean, the guys were good."

"Yeah, but you know they barely practised," Sasha reminded her. "Don't worry, all our hard work will definitely pay off."

"Sorry it didn't work out," Yasmin said when the boys returned to the audience to wait with their friends.

"What are you talking about?" Dylan cried. "I got 10 girls' phone

numbers – it couldn't have gone better than that!"

"Unless you'd got 11 phone numbers," Jade teased.

"Hey, I don't want to be greedy," he replied.

The girls just laughed, then sat back to listen to the rest of the auditions. They watched dozens of bands take the stage, some awful, some pretty good, but each time, the judges dismissed the group.

"They're not going to pick anyone from Stilesville!" Cloe wailed when every group except the Chix and the Starz had performed.

"Yeah, but they'll pick someone from Pleasant Grove!" Ashleigh vowed, strutting towards the stage with her friends. "Just watch!"

The Chix sounded even better than they had the previous weekend and their fans filled the auditorium with their enthusiastic cheers.

"That was fantastic," Evan declared.

"You've really got the Groove sound," Ian agreed.

"Can't wait to see you for round two in Chicago!" Carmen added.

"Yes!" the Chix cried, jumping up and down in excitement. They ran off the stage and stared smugly at the Starz.

"Beat that," Ally said.

"Oh, we intend to," Sasha replied.

The girls headed for the stage and launched into 'My Attitude' once more. Sasha's voice was rich and full of feeling, while her best friends added sparkling backing vocals and soaring instrumental accompaniment.

It hadn't seemed possible, but their fans were even louder than those who had cheered for the Chix and by the time the song ended, the entire audience was on their feet – all except Aimee, Ashleigh and Ally.

"Fabulous!" Evan declared.

"Perfect!" Ian agreed.

"See you in Chicago, girls!" Carmen added.

She gave the Starz a little wave, remembering them from Sasha's radio show, and they waved back excitedly.

"Okay, thank you everyone," Carmen announced. "We're really thrilled that all of you came out for our audition. But for now, it would be great if we could clear the auditorium so we can meet our finalists."

As the audience members and other bands made their way outside, Carmen motioned the Chix and the Starz towards the stage.

"Outta our way!" Ally snapped, shoving Yasmin aside as they climbed the steps onto the stage.

"Hey!" Yasmin gasped, stumbling.

"Whoops!" Ashleigh cried. "Watch your step!"

The girls glared at each other as they sat down in a semicircle around Carmen.

"We'll be flying all of you to Chicago tomorrow, where you'll audition in front of my business partner and the president of Groove, Max Maxwell," Carmen explained. "We've both picked our finalists from around the country, so you'll be competing against all our top picks there. We'll narrow it down from there until we have our grand prize winner. How does that sound, girls?"

"Fabulous!" chorused Cloe, Jade, Sasha and Yasmin.

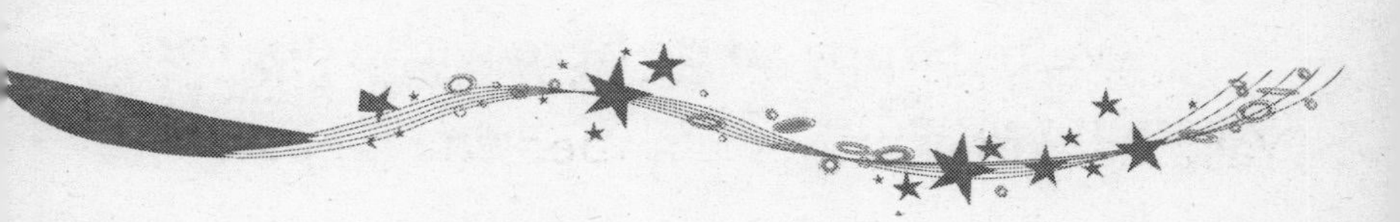

CHAPTER 11

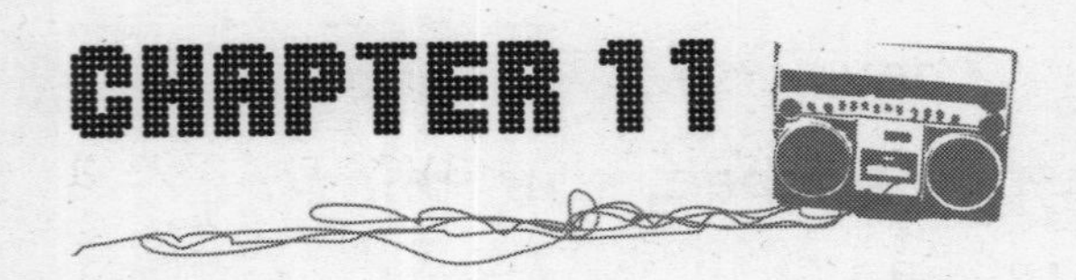

"What an incredible city," Cloe gushed as they rode through Chicago in Groove Records' limousine, on the way to their audition at Navy Pier.

"It does have a gorgeous skyline," Jade agreed.

"And a spectacular lakefront," Yasmin added.

"Girls, I'm so glad we could all be here together," Sasha declared. "And no matter what happens today, I am absolutely thrilled that I got this chance to perform with my three best friends in the world."

"Aww!" the girls cried and then burst into giggles.

"We're happy to be here with you, too," Yasmin replied.

At the pier, they scoped out the giant Ferris wheel, impressed. "We have to take a ride on that!" Cloe declared.

"We'll have plenty of time for sightseeing after the audition," Sasha reminded her.

"Not if we win!" Cloe protested. "If we win, we'll be whisked to Los Angeles to record our album, then start hitting every major city in the country on our tour!"

"Wow, poor us," Jade said dryly.

"Okay, you're right, that would be pretty awesome," Cloe admitted.

"Fingers crossed!" Yasmin exclaimed.

They headed for the Crystal Ballroom where the auditions were being held.

They were up last again, so they sat listening to a series of bands and watched as Carmen and Max dismissed them all. Soon only the Chix and the Starz remained, once again.

"Well, it looks like it's all up to you girls," Carmen declared. "None of the other bands compared to the sound we heard from you guys yesterday. So whichever of you wins will be Groove Records' new artist!"

All seven girls squealed with excitement until Aimee elbowed Cloe in the side.

"I don't know what you're getting so excited about," she hissed. "That record deal is ours."

Yasmin glanced over and saw that Carmen had noticed this exchange – and she didn't look happy. But Yasmin and her friends watched as the Chix took the stage and gave yet another amazing performance.

"I want this so bad," Cloe whispered. "But I'm scared they might be better."

"No way!" Sasha declared. "Come on, let's make some beautiful music together."

The Starz took their turn on the stage, sounding just as fantastic as the Chix had. But when they returned to their seats while the judges conferred, they weren't at all sure that they'd been good enough. The four best friends sat in a row, each clasping the hand of the girl next to her.

After what seemed like forever, Carmen and Max stepped forward.

"I have to say, I've never seen a closer competition," Carmen began.

"Both groups had the type of sound we're looking for and you both gave awesome performances," Max added.

"But Groove isn't just about music," Carmen continued. "It's about the spirit behind that music." She turned to the Chix.

"You're a very talented group of girls," she told them.

"Thanks," Aimee replied, shooting the Starz a smug look.

"But your attitude is off," Carmen told them. "I overheard some of the comments you made to your fellow competitors at the first auditions and I heard more today. And I have to tell you, as good as you are, that is not the attitude we want representing our label."

"Musically, it was a tie," Max explained. "But in terms of attitude, there's no beating these shining Starz!"

Cloe, Jade, Sasha and Yasmin turned to each other, stunned. They'd dreamed of winning, but they hadn't dared to believe until this moment that this deal could actually be theirs!

"Congratulations, girls," Carmen said. "And welcome to Groove Records!"

"Whatever," Ally muttered. She and her friends stalked off in a huff.

"I can't say I'm sad to see them go," Jade admitted.

"They were really good performers," Yasmin said.

"Too bad they had to be so mean!" Cloe added.

Carmen strode up to the Starz, a huge smile on her face.

"I was hoping you girls would win, you know," she said.

"Really?" Cloe asked.

"Absolutely!" Carmen replied. "I loved your enthusiasm that first day back at Stiles High and I could tell right away what an amazing team you four made."

"We really do, don't we?" Sasha said, slinging her arms around her best friends.

"And now, you're a part of the Groove

team!" Carmen declared. "So, girls, are you ready to head to Hollywood? We'll give you makeovers and a new wardrobe to prepare you for your tour. Then we'll record your album, do a few publicity shoots and interviews with the hippest magazines and then you'll give your first Groove concert in LA. From there, you'll tour 20 cities across the country, with a grand finale in New York. How does that sound?"

"You had me at 'makeover'," Jade replied. "But the rest sounds awesome, too."

"You know, I think you girls are going to fit right in with the Groove team!" Carmen announced. "Now come on, you have a plane to catch!"

Carmen and Max strode towards the door and Cloe, Jade and Yasmin started to follow. But Sasha held out her hand to stop them.

"What's wrong, Sash?" Cloe asked.

"Absolutely nothing," Sasha replied. She looked at each of her best friends in turn, a serious expression on her face. "I just wanted to thank you for making my dream come true."

"You made ours come true, too," Yasmin pointed out.

"Hey, that's what friends are for!" Jade declared.

Laughing, the girls slung their arms around each others' shoulders and headed for the door and the start of their spectacular pop-music career!

Read more about the Bratz in these other awesome books!

Pixie Power

Spring Break Safari

Diamond Road Trip

BRATZ Magazine

The magazine for girls with a **PASSION** for fashion!

ALL THE LATEST BRATZ & CELEBRITY NEWS!

ALL THE BEST FASHION TIPS & ADVICE!

COOL FEATURES, COMPETITIONS, POSTERS & MORE!

U.K. Customers get 1 issue free!
13 issues for only £29.25
Order online www.titanmagazines.co.uk/bratz
or call 0870 428 8206 (Quoting ref BRZPA1)

U.S. Customers Save 35%!
6 issues for only $19.50
Order online www.titanmagazines.com/bratz
or call 1 877 363 1310 (Quoting ref BRZPA2)